For word lovers and bird lovers.

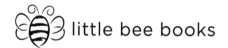

little bee books

An imprint of Bonnier Publishing Group
853 Broadway, New York, New York 10003
Copyright ©2016 by Bethanie Deeney Murguia
All rights reserved, including the right of reproduction
in whole or in part in any form. LITTLE BEE BOOKS is a
trademark of Bonnier Publishing Group, and associated colophon is
a trademark of Bonnier Publishing Group.
Manufactured in China LEO 0815
First Edition
2 4 6 8 10 9 7 5 3 1
Library of Congress Cataloging-in-Publication Data
is available upon request.
ISBN 978-1-4998-0102-6

littlebeebooks.com
bonnierpublishing.com

COCKATOO, TOO

COCKATOO, TOO

Bethanie Deeney Murguia

little bee books

Cockatoo.

Cockatoo two?

Cockatoo, too?

Two cockatoos!

Two cockatoos, too?

Cockatoo tutus!

Two cockatoo tutus, too?

Cockatoo tutus, too!

Two...

toucans.

Tutued toucans.

Tutued toucans can-can.

Can cockatoos can-can, too?

Yes.

Can-can you?